The Sea Pony

Krista Ruepp

The Sea Pony

Illustrated by Ulrike Heyne

Translated by J. Alison James

North-South Books

NEW YORK / LONDON

Copyright © 2001 by Nord-Süd Verlag AG, Gossau Zürich, Switzerland
First published in Switzerland under the title *Meerpony*
English translation copyright © 2001 by North-South Books Inc.

First published in the United States, Great Britain, Canada,
Australia, and New Zealand in 2001 by North-South Books,
an imprint of Nord-Süd Verlag AG, Gossau Zürich, Switzerland.

Distributed in the United States by North-South Books Inc., New York.

Library of Congress Cataloging-in-Publication Data is available.
A CIP catalogue record for this book is available from The British Library.
ISBN 0-7358-1534-8 (trade binding)
1 3 5 7 9 TB 10 8 6 4 2
ISBN 0-7358-1535-6 (library binding)
1 3 5 7 9 LB 10 8 6 4 2
Printed in Belgium

For more information about our books, and the authors and artists
who create them, visit our web site: www.northsouth.com

Contents

The New Boy

There was a new family on Outhorn Island. They had moved into an old farmhouse with a thatched roof. It was set back in a meadow of wildflowers and fruit trees. The family had a boy. His name was Philip.

Every bit of news about the new family was told around the village. It wasn't often that people moved to the island.

Charlie was on her way to school one morning when she saw Matthew Grimm, the man who owned the horse she rode.

"Hello, Charlie!" he called out. "Have you heard? The new people have brought a pony with them."

"I know," she said. "It belongs to Philip. He'll be in my class."

"That pony acts strangely," said Mr. Grimm. "Every evening he stands all alone on the dune at the edge of the pasture and stares sadly out at the ocean."

"That is strange," said Charlie. "Why do you think he does that?"

Mr. Grimm shrugged his shoulders.

Then the school bell rang, and Charlie raced off to class. "See you this afternoon," she called.

In her class she met Philip.

Philip was nine years old, the same as
Charlie. He was a bit shy. His hair was all
bristly. It framed his narrow face. His dark
eyes and his serious mouth gave him a
very thoughtful expression.

Charlie was an island girl. Actually her name was Charlotte, but everyone called her Charlie. She had red, shaggy hair, a stub nose, and thousands of freckles.

"Where did you live before you moved here?" she asked Philip.

"I lived at the edge of a forest high in the mountains. All there is here is sea and grass." Philip looked sadly out of the window.

"Don't you like it here?" Charlie asked.

"No," Philip answered.

"Maybe once you get used to it you'll like it better," said Charlie. "You have a pony. We can go riding together sometime. I'll show you the island."

"No, that's okay. I don't feel like it. My pony doesn't like it here either," he said.

He's crazy, Charlie thought, and turned away.

Homesick

Charlie's best friend was Starbright, a
white stallion. Matthew Grimm was glad
that Charlie took such good care of his
horse. She was allowed to ride him
whenever she wanted.

That afternoon when Charlie was out
riding, she saw Philip in the meadow.
He was feeding his pony hay and carrots.

"Hello, Philip," Charlie called.

"Oh, it's you," said the boy.

Charlie got off Starbright, tied her reins
to the fence, and went over to Philip.

"What's your pony's name?" asked Charlie.

"Goblin," answered Philip.

"Funny name," said Charlie.

"He comes from Iceland," Philip said. "They named him that because he was always playing tricks. Once he nipped a man in the backside. And he was always stealing hats from children."

Charlie laughed. "Does he still do stuff like that?"

"No. Since he's been with us, he hasn't played tricks at all."

Philip's parents had given him the pony as a present just before they moved to the island. Goblin was golden brown. He had a white tail and a long, white mane.

It grew late. The rays of the setting sun danced like tiny beads of light on the waves. On the horizon the evening clouds shone red and gold. Slowly the sun sank into the sea.

Goblin trotted up the dune and looked out across the ocean.

Charlie ran after him.

Goblin seemed to smell something from far beyond the horizon. Greedily he breathed in the salty sea air.

Slowly it grew dark. Philip climbed up on the dune, too. He and Charlie sat together in the grass.

"I just want to move back home," Philip said.

"Why? It's so beautiful here!"

"But at home there are the mountains, and the forest . . . and all my friends. Here I don't have anyone. . . ."

"You have Goblin. And anyway, you haven't been here all that long," said Charlie, trying to comfort him.

A Million Stars

Charlie let herself fall back and tucked her arms under her head. "A million stars!"

Philip looked at the sky.

Over them the stars glittered like diamonds on dark velvet.

"Nowhere in the world is the sky anywhere near this beautiful," whispered Charlie.

The children didn't notice how time was passing.

The wind had died down. Only the sound of the surf could be heard from a distance. Soon the moon rose in the sky and bathed the land in soft light.

Suddenly the children heard a rustling noise in the grass. Somebody was coming right toward them!

"Oh, it's you!" cried Charlie, relieved.

It was Old Fig, a fisherman from the village. He often walked the dunes and the beach at night.

"So here you are, Charlie," said Old Fig. "Your parents are looking for you. And yours, too, boy. . . ."

Old Fig gave a quick nod and went on his way.

"I'd better hurry," said Philip, leaping to his feet.

"Do you want to go riding tomorrow?" asked Charlie.

"Okay."

"Then let's meet here at four," suggested Charlie. She turned Starbright and rode off in the darkness.

Philip left Goblin in the meadow and ran home.

"Where have you been?" his mother asked when Philip came through the door.

"I was with Goblin. And then this girl Charlie came by. She's in my class. She has a horse, too," Philip said. "And then we sat on the dunes."

"Sounds like a nice girl, this Charlie," his mother said.

Charlie's parents also wanted to know why she'd been out so late. She told them about Philip, about Goblin, and about the million stars.

That night, Charlie lay awake for a long time. How would I feel if I had to move away from Outhorn? she wondered. What would I do without the sea and the dunes, without my friends? What if all I had were mountains and forests around me? And what if I didn't even have Starbright? Awful! At least Philip has Goblin. Tomorrow I'll show him the island, and maybe he'll start to like it here. He's really quite nice, that Philip....

Then she fell asleep.

Island Ride

The next afternoon they met as planned. The sun shone. A strong west wind chased little white clouds across the sky. It was a wonderful island day.

When Starbright discovered the pony, he trotted over to him. The two horses sniffed each other nervously. Then they whinnied and stamped their forelegs.

Philip had Goblin saddled already, so the children rode off.

"I'll show you the moor," said Charlie.

The moor began right behind the
dunes. It was covered with brightly
glowing heather.

The moor smelled of the wild herbs
and flowers that grew there.

"We have to stay on the path," Charlie
called. "Rare plants grow all over the
place here."

"Look at that!" cried Philip. "The
gentians are in bloom. We have them in
the mountains."

Charlie showed him other flowers:
chicory, daisy, bellflower, and arnica.

They stopped the horses.

Crickets and grasshoppers chirped in
the heather, and high above sang skylarks.

They trotted farther toward the marsh.
Sheep grazed on both sides of the path.

"Race you to the sea!" Charlie called.
She urged Starbright on.

Goblin followed close on their heels,
but he never managed to pass Starbright.

A pair of ravens flew cawing overhead. The thunder of the hooves had startled them.

Soon the children reached the beach. The waves had white foam peaks. Seagulls circled and drifted across the sky on the wind.

"Faster!" cried Charlie, and the horses sped away. In a wild gallop they splashed along the water's edge. Goblin grew so spirited that Philip could hardly hold him.

The air tasted of salt, and it smelled of algae, almost like Goblin's home in Iceland. Under the horses' hooves the water sprayed high.

Great Danger

The horses ran faster and faster. When they reached the end of the beach, they stopped. They puffed and snorted, because the saltwater tickled their nostrils.

For the first time, Philip laughed. "That was totally fantastic!"

"Hey, you can laugh," said Charlie.

But then Goblin pranced around restlessly. Indignantly, he shook his mane. Then he reared up on his hind legs.

"Something's wrong with him!" Philip cried.

"Try to calm him down!"

Goblin turned in circles.

Philip looked anxiously at Charlie. "He's crazy. He wants to run again!"

Philip pulled on the reins, but Goblin didn't stop. He plowed through the little waves and then went straight on into the deep water. Philip dropped the reins and grabbed Goblin's neck with both arms.

Little waves splashed against Goblin's chest.

"What are you doing? Bring him back!" Charlie called.

But Goblin just drove on farther, into the big waves, into the ocean.

A huge breaker rose in front of them. Goblin ducked his head and leapt right into it. He came up swimming.

"Are you out of your mind?" Charlie yelled. She'd never seen anything like this before. I have to go for help! she thought, and looked around. But there was nobody to be seen. She couldn't just leave them.

Goblin and Philip were already beyond the breakers where the water rose and fell in great gentle swells. Goblin swam with powerful strokes straight toward the north.

I have to help them! Charlie urged
Starbright on. "We've got to bring them
back!" she cried. Starbright balked.
Charlie dug her heels into Starbright's
flanks. Trembling, they both headed into
the water.

A giant wave curled towards them.

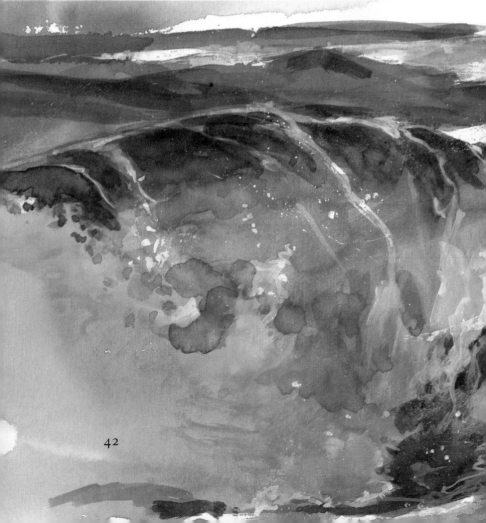

Charlie pressed herself against Starbright's back and held her breath. The wave broke. They swam under and through. Then the water was calmer, and Starbright could swim easily. He was a big horse, and slowly they were able to gain on the other two.

"Philip!" Charlie cried.

Starbright tried to cut the pony off.

Wild panic shone in Goblin's eyes.

Philip screamed, "Help me, Charlie! Help!"

"Hold on tight!" she cried to him. "We'll make it!"

But it wasn't so easy.

Goblin wouldn't be stopped by
Starbright; he just kept swimming.

"Quick, loosen up one of your reins!
Good! Now throw it here!"

Charlie caught Goblin's rein and tugged
on it, as hard as she could. Reluctantly,
Goblin turned to follow Starbright.

The children swam back with the
horses. At the breaker line, a big wave
lifted them up and rushed them toward
the shore.

The wave crashed over them when it broke, and the children were spewed out like shipwrecked sailors and washed up on the beach.

Exhausted but relieved, they waded to dry ground. They coughed and sneezed because they'd swallowed so much water.

"You saved my life, Charlie," said Philip, shivering and gasping for breath.

"Well, I couldn't just let you two swim away." Charlie laughed and clapped Philip on the shoulder.

"Come on," she said. "We can go to the Ocean Rescue Station. It's equipped for shipwrecks."

Charlie knew the station was filled with sirens, lifeboats, and radio equipment. It also was the best place for them to get warm and dry.

The children tied the horses outside and went in.

The Sea Pony

"What happened to you two?" The man from the station was shocked at the sight of the cold, dripping children. "Did you fall in the water, Charlie?"

They told him what happened while he made them hot chocolate and gave them heavy pullovers to wear until their clothes got dry.

"I just couldn't hold Goblin back," said Philip.

Charlie was very thoughtful. "He was so determined, as if he knew exactly where he was going. What do you suppose he wanted out there in the middle of the ocean?"

Philip just shook his head.

After a while, the two of them were
warm enough to ride back home.

First they took Starbright back to his stable. They were rubbing down both horses when Matthew Grimm came in.

"What happened to you two?" he asked.

The children told him the story.

"You know what?" Philip said. "He swam in the same direction that he looks at when he stands on top of the dunes."

"How strange," said Mr. Grimm.

Charlie asked, "Isn't Iceland north of here? That's where Goblin came from."

Mr. Grimm nodded. "It's northwest. And when I've seen that pony on the dunes, he is facing almost exactly northwest. I'll bet he has a bad case of homesickness. Horses take time to get used to new surroundings."

"I thought only people got homesick," Philip said.

"Goblin left all his friends, too," Charlie said. "And he is all alone out there on the moor."

"Why don't you leave Goblin here with
Starbright for a while," said Mr. Grimm.

"You mean it?" Philip asked, his eyes
shining. "You have room for him?"

"That would be fantastic!" said Charlie.
"Then at least he'll have a friend."

They led Goblin and Starbright out to
the pasture, slapped their rumps and let
them run.

Philip was grinning. "I hope they'll get
along," he said.

"Look at how well they're doing
already," Mr. Grimm said.

Goblin nipped Starbright in the flank.
Starbright snorted and ran a short way
off. In high spirits, Goblin ran behind.
And soon they stood near each other and
grazed like old friends.

"He played a trick!" Philip said quietly.
"He hasn't done that since he left
Iceland."

A Gift for Charlie

The children met the next afternoon.

"What did your parents say last night?" Charlie wanted to know.

"My father was angry. He said that if Goblin goes into the ocean like that again, then we'll have to give him up."

They didn't dare ride on the beach again for several days after that.

But then there was an afternoon when the wind was calm and the sun was hot and the scent of heather lay heavy in the air. Charlie and Philip couldn't resist.

"Come on," Charlie said, "Let's see who's first to the big dune!"

"Yippie!" Philip hooted. "I'll win this time for sure!" Goblin thundered past Starbright at full gallop.

Goblin ran the length of the beach and didn't seem to notice the sea. Had he forgotten his homesickness?

Out of breath, they stopped the horses at the big dune.

"You are the best, Philip," Charlie said, panting.

"You, too," said Philip. For the first time they looked each other in the eyes, and that made them laugh.

Philip slipped off Goblin, bent over to the sand, and then held his fist up to Charlie. "For you," he said, and he opened his hand slowly—a perfect scallop shell.

"It's beautiful," said Charlie. "Thanks!"

"I guess there are some nice things about this island after all," said Philip, and then they both laughed again.

About the Author

Krista Ruepp was born in Cologne, Germany. After studying to be a teacher, she worked as an editor for a German television network, then in advertising and marketing. For young readers, she has written stories, poetry, and songs. Her first book for North-South, *Midnight Rider*, introduced Charlie and the stallion Starbright. She now lives in Remschied, Germany, with her husband, their two sons, a dog, and an Arabian mare.

About the Illustrator

Ulrike Heyne was born in Dresden, Germany. She studied fashion illustration and graphic design in Munich, and then spent several years working in advertising and teaching painting and drawing. She illustrated two earlier books featuring Charlie and Starbright, both written by Krista Ruepp, *Midnight Rider* and *Horses in the Fog*. She lives with her husband in Possendorf, near Dresden, not far from the city where she was born.

Read more about Charlie
and her stallion, Starbright,
in *Midnight Rider* and
Horses in the Fog.

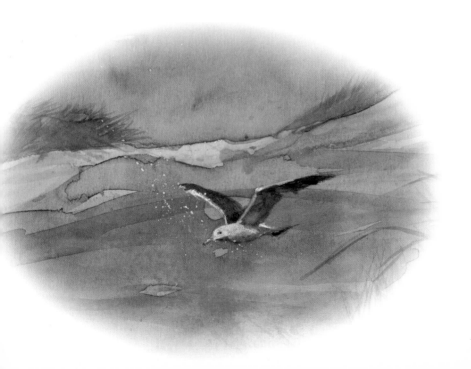